# God Is Good

# We Should

# Be

# Thankful

By Mrs. James Swartzentruber

Pictures by Daniel Zook and Lester Miller

## To the Teacher:

This book is designed to give constructive reading practice to pupils using the grade one *Bible Nurture and Reader Series.* It uses words that have been introduced in the reader or can be mastered with phonics skills taught by Unit 3, Lesson 30. A few new words also appear in the story, printed in italics. At the end of the book, these words are listed with pronunciations and / or illustrations to help the children to learn them on their own. Be sure the children understand that the words are vocabulary or sound words except the words in italics, and where to look to learn the new words if they need help. They should be able to read this book independently.

Books in this series with their placement according to reading and phonics lessons:

*Copyright, 1976*

By

**Rod and Staff Publishers, Inc.**
**Crockett, Kentucky 41413**
**Telephone (606) 522-4348**

Printed in U.S.A.

ISBN 978-07399-0065-9

Catalog no. 2257

14    15    16    17    18    —    21    20    19    18    17    16    15    14    13    12

"Kathy," Mother called up the stairway, "it is time to get up."

"Yes," came a sleepy voice from upstairs.

Kathy rolled over and got out

of bed. She knelt to pray and then dressed. But she did not dress quickly as she did other mornings.

Picking up her *shoes* and stockings, she went slowly down the stairs.

Kathy did not put on her *shoes* and stockings right away. She just sat there for a while. She pulled on one stocking and then rested a little while again before pulling on the other one.

"Kathy, where are you?" called Mother. She could not

understand why it took so long for Kathy to come this morning.

"I will come soon," said

Kathy as she tied her *shoes*.

Kathy washed her face and hands. Her face did not feel right. Her cheeks felt big. It hurt below her ears. She wiped her face and hands and then went to help Mother.

"Good morning, Kathy," said Mother.

Then Mother looked again. "Kathy," she said, "I think you must have the mumps! I don't think you feel very well. You will not need to help me this morning.

You may go and lie down."

Kathy did indeed have the mumps. All day she felt sick, and the next, and the next, and the next day, too. Most of the time she rested.

After Kathy was not feeling so sick anymore, Mother said she could be up more.

Sometimes Kathy looked at books. Sometimes she colored in her new coloring book. Sometimes she read stories from *Wee Lambs* to her little brother, Samuel, who also had the mumps now.

But one morning Kathy was feeling grouchy. She had lost her sunny smile.

She did not feel like looking at books or reading to Samuel.

She did not feel like coloring in her new coloring book.

She did not feel like cutting out pictures to paste into her scrapbook. She felt very unhappy.

"Mother, when may I go outside again?" asked Kathy. "I wish I could go outside once."

Mother looked at Kathy. Where was her cheerful little girl? "I think you can soon play outside again," she said. "But we don't want you to go out too soon and get sick again. You would not like that, would you?"

Kathy shook her head. "I wish I would not have the mumps."

"But just think, Kathy," said Mother. "You have needed to stay in the house for only a week. Some children are sick for a long time.

"Remember when Donald broke his leg and could not walk for a long time?

"And you remember Joy's grandmother. She has been in a *wheelchair* for many years, but she always seems very happy. She says God is good to her."

"And like Grace," said Kathy. "She was sick a long time, too."

"No one has so much trouble that he cannot still be thankful," said Mother.

"Do you remember that verse we talked about one morning last week? It is the one Father said we should all learn: 'In every thing give thanks.'"

Kathy could not understand
that. "Does that mean I need to
thank God for mumps?" She did
not think she could do that!

Mother smiled. "Even though you have the mumps, you should still be thankful for the many good things God does for you.

"There is a verse that says we shall give thanks <u>for</u> all things. You can even be thankful for the mumps.

"If we are sick, it helps us to know how others feel when they are sick. It helps us to be kind to them. It helps us in other ways, too.

"We can thank God for everything because He takes care of us."

Kathy stood at the window and looked outside. A week seemed like a long time. She surely was glad it would not need to be weeks and weeks. How she would love to go outside again!

The grass was getting nice and green. She remembered how good it felt to her bare feet.

But she did not think Mother would want her to go barefoot for a while yet.

A white kitten and a yellow kitten were playing with something in the grass.

Kathy looked up into the big oak tree. Why was that *squirrel* chattering so?

He was looking in the direction of the road and scolding long and loud. His tail looked like a big ?, and it jerked back and forth very fast while he scolded.

Kathy looked to see what he saw, and there inside the fence sat a big black cat!

Then Kathy saw something else.

A small brown bird was
flying to the little birdhouse on
the porch post. It was carrying a
short stick in its beak.

Kathy watched the little
brown wren. It went into the hole
in the little house.

Soon the bird came out again, but it did not have the short stick in its beak any more. It was bringing things to make a cozy little nest in the little house.

Soon it was back with another small stick. It went into the little house. Then it came out

and flew away again.

After a while the wren came back with a bigger stick in its beak.

"I wonder how it will get that into such a little hole?" thought Kathy.

It tried and tried to get the

stick in. Then the stick fell to the ground.

"Now it will look for something else," thought Kathy.

But the little wren did not go to look for something else. It flew down, picked up the same stick, and tried again. It tried to push the stick in one way and then another. Soon it fell again.

The little wren flew down, picked it up with its sharp little beak, and tried again.

Again the little brown wren tried, and tried, and tried, but it could not get the stick to go into the small hole in the little house. The stick fell again.

This time the wren left the stick and flew to a nearby tree.

"Now it will sit there and scold," thought Kathy. But it did not.

What do you think the little wren did? It sat on a limb and sang and sang!

"The wren isn't unhappy because it cannot do what it would like to do," thought Kathy. "It sings because it is happy."

Watching the wren made Kathy feel ashamed for feeling so grouchy. Even though she could not run out to play, she could still be thankful.

Kathy started to think of the many things for which she could be thankful.

"I can still see. Some children

are blind and cannot see at all. They cannot see the nice green grass, the blue sky, the moon and the many stars at night, or the pretty flowers, the animals, and the birds. They cannot even see their families!

"I can hear, too." Kathy loved to hear the birds sing, the pit-pat of rain on the roof, the wind blowing through the pine trees, kind words, and, oh, so many things!

"I have wonderful parents," thought Kathy. "They love me. They punish me when I am bad. They help me to do what is right. Some children have parents that do not love God and are not kind to their families.

"I live in a good home and have a warm, cozy bed. Some children do not have even a bed to sleep in or warm covers to cover them when it is cold.

"I always have enough to eat." Kathy knew there were many people who did not have enough food to eat.

"Oh, there are so many things to thank God for!" thought Kathy with a smile.

Soon Mother heard Kathy humming a happy tune while she colored in her new coloring book. She was still thinking about the many things for which to be thankful.

How many things can you name for which you are thankful?

shoes (shōoz)

squirrel (skwėr·ul)

wheelchair (whēl·chār)